SARAI

IN THE SPOTLIGHT!

SARAI GONZALEZ
AND
MONICA BROWN

SCHOLASTIC INC.

ISBN 978-1-338-23669-9

10 9 8 7 6 5 4 3 2 1   18 19 20 21 22

Printed in the U.S.A.   40

First printing 2018

Book design by Carolyn Bull

To my awesome best friend,
Samantha!
-SG

For Maya Isabel, who is
beautiful and strong.
-MB

CONTENTS

INTRODUCTION

I, SARAI

I, Sarai, am happy. Not just happy. Awesome! The sun is shining through the window. I get out from under my cozy covers and get up to start the day. I'm the first one up, which is how I like it. Mom, Dad, and my two little sisters, Josie and Lucía, are still asleep. Today is going to rock. As in, I will rock it!

I can't wait for school because I want to tell my best friend Isa Lopez all about my adventures. She went on a trip with her family, and I haven't seen her in over a week. It's kind of weird because we haven't been on spring break or anything. I

haven't been able to share my big news, which is that my grandparents—Tata and my Mama Rosi—just bought a house a couple of blocks away from me. And, even better, they bought it together with my cousins' family! Now my Tía Sofía, my Tío Miguel, and my three cousins, JuJu, Javier, and Jade, live super close to us, and I get to see the Js all the time!

I thought JuJu would be going to my school, but her parents are sending her to the Catholic school instead. It doesn't matter, though, because the important thing is that we are close. I want my super best cousin, JuJu, to meet my super best school friend, Isa.

Isa has a business just like me. My business is Sarai's Sweets, and I make cupcakes. Isa has Isa's Eats, and she makes great Mexican food with her mom, who she's named after. They sell tamales and enchiladas at church during the holidays and on special Sundays, and we always buy lots. When we get older, Isa and I are going to go into business together. I'm sure Isa will be back today because it's Monday and people come back to school on Mondays. Today is going to be GREAT.

CHAPTER 1

ALARM BUNNY

I sneak out of my room, careful not to make noise. I love it when I'm the first one up. I grab my stuffed bunny and walk across the hall to my sisters' room. I get down on all fours and crawl toward the bed so Lucía can't see me, and I hold the bunny up over my head and near Lucía's ear.

"Luuuuuuuuuuuuuuucía," I say in my bunny voice, "alarm bunny says it's time to WAKE UP!" I yell the last part, and then I tickle her. She yells, jumps up out of bed, and climbs into Josie's bed and pulls the covers over her head for protection.

I tickle both my sisters until I am sure they are awake. We make so much noise, so I know my parents must be awake now too.

"You are so silly, Sarai!" my sister Josie signs and says. Josie is deaf. She has special implants that help her hear sounds. She uses a combination of signs and words to communicate. Lucía and Josie start jumping from bed to bed, which is one of their favorite games. I don't even try to stop them because when I do, Lucía says "It's not your job to boss us," and then she jumps even higher.

I go to my room to get dressed for the day. I feel sparkly, so I put on my favorite jeans and a pink shirt that says "Girls Rock!" in glittery letters. I lace up my pink high-tops and grab my purple jacket for later.

"Come and eat, girls!" my dad says, poking his head into our rooms. "We've got pizza and ice cream for breakfast!"

"What?" I say, and race out of my room.

"Just kidding!" he says. My dad thinks he's pretty funny.

There's toast on the table and Mom is frying eggs, and it feels like the start of a good week.

Dad and Josie leave early to make the long drive to her school. It's a school for deaf and hearing-impaired children. They spend a long time in the car each way, but it's worth it because Dad says Josie deserves the best education in the world—that we all do. The teachers at Josie's school sign, speak and demonstrate in action what they teach. Lucía and I go to Martin Luther King, Jr. Elementary, the public school nearby. Martin Luther King, Jr. is a hero who fought for equal rights for us all.

Mom and Dad say we should all be like Dr. King and stand for justice. After all, we are the Gonzalez five—Dad, Mom, Josie, Lucía, and me.

"I want you girls to stand up for yourselves," Mom always says, and I agree. Right when mom leaves for her job, Lucía and I leave to walk a block to the bus stop.

"Have a great day!" Mom always says before she leaves.

"You too!" I call back.

As soon as Lucía and I get to the bus stop, kids start talking to her. "Hi, Lucía!" they say, and "How are you?" and "Will you sit next to me on the bus?" She's super popular and has a lot of friends. I don't have as many, so it's kind of nice that Lucía always wants to sit next to me on the bus.

Lucía has a big imagination. That's a fact. Another fact is that she has a little bit of a temper. One year, for example, we didn't get a real Christmas tree. We just had a little plastic one because our apartment was so small. Lucía got so mad that she decided to draw a giant tree on the wall. She signed her name, Lucía G., right next to it. And she STILL tried to say, "Josie did it!" Whenever anyone tries to get Lucía to do something she doesn't want to do, she says, "You got to be kidding me!" even though we usually aren't.

When we get to school, Lucía goes off to the first-grade class and I head to my fourth-grade homeroom. Josie is in the second grade at her school.

I'm getting settled at my desk, when my teacher, Ms. Moro, says, "Sarai, come up to my desk for a minute. There's something I'd like to share with you." She sounds serious, and that makes me a little anxious, even though I know I haven't done anything wrong.

"Sarai," Ms. Moro says. "I have some unfortunate news. It looks like Isa Lopez won't be coming back to Martin Luther King, Jr. Elementary."

"What?" I say. "That's impossible. She's my super best friend, and she would have told me. Is she okay?"

"She's fine. I know it's surprising, but I have a letter for you here from Isa. Isa's father's work transferred him out of state, and everything happened in a rush, so she didn't get to say goodbye to her school friends." Ms. Moro smiles. "I know it seems terrible, Sarai, but you are an amazing girl, and there are lots of new friends to make. In fact, a brand-new student just enrolled. She'll be here tomorrow."

I don't care about new students or new friends, I think. I want Isa, my old and best friend. Some of the girls in my class are kind of mean, to be honest, and it's always been Isa and me against the world—or at least in our own world. Isa and I have so much in common. We both like pink and sparkles, and singing, dancing, and acting, and cooking. I take the letter from Ms. Moro and walk back to my desk. I open the letter. It reads:

 Dear Sarai,

I can't believe I'm moving, or actually, by the time you read this, already moved. My dad got a new job all the way in Washington, D.C., and my parents didn't want to pay for two rents, so we had to move right away. I miss you already. Now I have to go to a new school with all new people. I hope everyone is nice, but even if they are, it won't be the same because YOU won't be there. The only good thing is that now we can be pen pals. I've always wanted a pen pal! And maybe you can visit me in Washington, D.C., some day. There are lots of cool monuments. My parents say there is even one of Martin Luther King, Jr., the person our school is named after!

From your super best (long-distance) friend,

Isa

P.S. My new address is on the back of this envelope. Write back soon and tell me what's new.

Oh no, I think. What am I going to do?

CHAPTER 2

CAFETERIA TROUBLES

When I walk into the cafeteria, I see there are a few spots at my usual table. By usual table, I mean the table that Isa and I always sat at. I set my backpack down in a seat and then go to get my food. Lucía is waiting for me in the lunch line. I have the cafeteria card with the money on it. Lucía used to have her own cafeteria card, but she kept buying food for everyone who she thought didn't have enough to eat and the money

would run out in two days. Now I pay for both our lunches with my card.

"How's your day going?" I ask Lucía.

"Great!" she says.

"Good!" I say. I like lunch because there's always an interesting menu at school. Interesting can be good or bad, but today it's good. It's never as good as the Peruvian food my mom and my grandmother Mama Rosi make. My other grandmother, my

Mama Chila, makes yummy Costa Rican food for us too, sometimes. But she and my Papá live farther away, so we don't get to see them as often. My dad was born in Costa Rica and my mom was born in Peru, but now everyone's together here in the United States, where my sisters and I were born. My mom says we are citizens of the world.

Today they have chicken fingers and milk and fruit salad, which is my favorite way to eat fruit. Of course, this fruit salad doesn't look like my mom's. She puts in every kind of fruit in the universe and then adds a little cinnamon. Still, I

like the bright red cherries in the cafeteria's salad. They taste like candy. After I pay for our lunch, Lucía is off to eat with her friends.

I hear her say, "After lunch, let's play kickball!"

That's my sister, I think, smiling. She loves to compete, and she's really strong. She's almost as tall as me already! When I get to my table, my smile disappears. Someone has moved my backpack. Again. It's been happening off and on all week— ever since Isa left. I didn't mind that much before because I knew Isa would be back soon and we'd laugh about it. If she were with me right now, she'd march over and move my backpack right back to where it was, and dare anyone to try and stop her. But now that I know she's not going to come back, I need to decide what to do.

"Who moved my stuff?" I say to the table. No one answers, but I'm pretty sure it's this girl named Valéria because she's been bothering me since the second grade. Once, when I was feeling extra awesome, I put in my most colorful ribbons and loved what I saw in the mirror. But when I got to school, Valéria walked up to me in front of everyone and said, "Sarai, you look like a space alien." Then she laughed.

"Sarai looks awesome," I remember Isa said.

"Who cares what *you* think anyway?" I told Valéria. "It's *my* hair." But the truth is that I did care what she thought, just a little. Instead of feeling good I felt like everyone was staring at me and laughing behind my back.

Now I look up and down the table and say again, "Who moved my backpack? Where is it?" Valéria and her friends just stare at me. Valéria has lots of friends and lots of clothes too. It seems like she wears a new outfit every day. Her friend Kayla giggles, and I can't tell if it's a nervous giggle or a mean giggle. Kayla and I used to be pretty friendly before she started hanging out with Valéria. I take a deep breath.

"You're not allowed to move my stuff," I say. "Give me my backpack or I'll go tell a teacher."

"You're such a tattletale," Valéria says and I hear someone say, "Baby." Then Valéria stands up and points under the table, and she and her friends move tables. I look under the table, and there's my pink backpack, on the floor getting dirty.

"Really?" Ms. Milligan asks.

"Well, I always read right before bed," I explain. "And then sometimes I dream about the stories I'm reading."

"That's wonderful!" Ms. Milligan says, smiling. "But we'd better not get you scary stories if they show up in your dreams."

"That's okay," I tell Ms. Milligan, "because I like all types of books and I'm not afraid of anything!" And then I'm off, walking up and down the library stacks looking for books. The best part about our fourth-grade class being attached to the middle school is that our library is HUGE! I could check out ten books a week and *still* not get through all these books before I graduate. I pick out books for myself but also a few for my sisters. I even find a book about Hawaii for Lucía. She saw a movie set in Hawaii, and ever since, she's been dying to go.

I make sure I'm the last person in my class to check out books so I can talk with Ms. Milligan one more time.

"I didn't tell you the whole truth," I tell her.

"You didn't tell me the whole truth about what?" Ms. Milligan asks, looking concerned.

"Well, when I said I wasn't afraid of anything, that wasn't exactly true," I say. "Because now that Isa left, I'm afraid that I won't ever have a super best school friend again."

"Yes, I heard the Lopez family left. That must

be really hard for you, Sarai. I know you and Isa were really close. I can see you feel sad, but I know you'll make some new friends soon," Ms. Milligan says.

"I hope so," I say.

"I know so," Ms. Milligan says back. "In fact, I have an idea about that . . ."

I'm about to ask Ms. Milligan what her idea is when the bell rings, and I realize I need to go or I'll be late getting back to Ms. Moro's class.

CHAPTER 3

BOOM!

On our bus ride home, I give Lucía the Hawaii book. She is so excited! When we get to our house, Tata is waiting on the porch as usual. My grandfather watches us until Dad and Josie and Mom get home. Today Tata's playing with what looks like a big black plastic box.

"Hola, Tata!" I say.

"What's that?" asks Lucía.

"It's an old boom box," he says. "I got it at a garage sale last weekend for only eight dollars. It's not working right now, but I know I can fix it."

"Boom box?" I ask. "Does it go *boom*?"

"Like fireworks?" asks Lucía.

"No," Tata says, laughing. "It plays music with cassette tapes." Then he shows us a stack of little plastic rectangles that are the size of a deck of cards. The outsides of the cassettes have words written on them.

"This one says 'Dance Party Mix'!" I say. "And here's one that says 'Queen of Salsa/King of Mambo.'"

"I'm a queen!" says Lucía! "Let's listen to that one."

"I'm the queen, and you're the princess," I tell Lucía.

"No you're not!" she says.

"Well, I'm oldest," I tell her, "and that's just how it works."

"Girls!" Tata says. "The queen on that tape is Celia Cruz, the Cuban singer. When I fix the boom box, we can have a dance party and you can both be reinas."

"The king of mambo was Tito Puente, a Puerto Rican drummer," Tata says. "When he played his timbales, his arms moved so fast they were a blur." Tata pulls two screwdrivers out of his toolbox and starts tapping out a beat on our porch railing.

"You're so good!" I tell Tata.

"But not as good as your Mama Rosi's food, which is waiting to be eaten. Let's go in and eat," Tata says. We follow Tata into the house, and he warms up arroz con pollo for us. He always brings over food that my grandmother makes, and we eat it after school. Today it's chicken and rice. I like the cilantro and red peppers.

"I want to perform like Celia and Tito," I say. "I already dance with my group, the Playful Primas, but I want to sing and act and play musical instruments . . ."

"You want to do everything!" Lucía laughs.

"And why can't I?" I ask.

"You can," Tata says, smiling.

That night, after dinner, when we are all sitting around the family room, talking about our day, I decide to tell my parents about what happened at school. I explain about Valéria and Kayla and their friends and how they moved my backpack and even called me a baby.

"That happened again? I'm sorry about that, Sarai," Mom says. "I was hoping it was a one-time thing. That isn't nice at all."

"That's mean!" Josie says and signs. She jumps up to give me a hug. She knows what it's like to be teased. Once, when we were at the park, a boy made fun of the way Josie talked and made her cry. I was so mad that my face got as hot as a chili pepper, and I yelled at him. My dad came running and so did the little boy's mom. When I explained what happened, the mom made the little boy apologize, but I still remember it. So does Josie.

"Whenever I do my hair in my special way, they laugh at me," I say.

"You've got to be kidding me!" Lucía says, standing up. "I'm going to get those girls." It's funny, Lucía, Josie, and I sometimes fight and disagree with each other, but we'll always stick up for each other—no matter what.

"No, Lucía," Dad says. "No one is going to *get* anyone else. We are going to talk this through."

"I don't need your help," I tell my sister. She's younger than me. I'm supposed to help *her*. "You can't make them like me."

"I feel sorry for those girls because they aren't giving themselves a chance to get to know you," Dad says.

"And I rock!" I say.

"You do!" Mom says. "I'm proud of you for standing up for yourself, Sarai, but it sounds like a lot to deal with. Maybe I should talk with your teacher."

"But I don't want the teacher to *make* them be nice to me. I want them to be nice on their own."

"I understand what you're saying," Dad says, "but that doesn't mean we can't help."

"Let me try to fix this myself," I say. "I don't want them to think I'm afraid of them."

"Asking for help doesn't mean you are afraid," Mom says. "It means you're brave. But we can see how the next few days go."

"Thanks," I say. But I want to try to handle it on my own. Even if I'm not sure exactly how yet.

CHAPTER 4

THE NEW GIRL

When I get to Ms. Moro's classroom, I can tell right away that something's different. For one, the desks are rearranged. Every month or so, Ms. Moro moves us around so that we sit next to different people for group work and so that we take turns getting to be in the front of the classroom. I look for my name tag on the desks in the front row. It's not there. I see that Valéria and her friend Kayla are in the first and second row, one behind the other. I keep looking. At least I'm not sitting next to them. I find my nameplate on

a desk in the very back row. I look to the right, and on the desk is a name I don't recognize. Christina. She must be the new girl that Ms. Moro mentioned yesterday.

A girl with red hair and lots of freckles walks in and sits down next to me. She's wearing jeans and a black sweatshirt. Her hair is short and her ears are pierced and she's wearing silver earrings that look like horses.

"Hi," I say. "Most people call me SAR-EYE, which rhymes with 'I.' My grandparents pronounce my name SAH-RAH-EE, which rhymes with 'me.' What's your name?" At first, the new girl just looks at me. Then she looks down at the nameplate on her desk.

"Oh, you're Christina," I say, "the new girl." She looks at me without saying anything. "I like your horse earrings."

"They're actually unicorns," she says quietly.

"Oh, now I see the horn!" I say. "Unicorns are cool, even if they aren't real."

"How do you know?" Christina asks in a voice so low I can hardly hear her, but just then Ms. Moro starts taking roll and Christina turns away from me in her seat. I look at her dark clothes and notice her fingernails. They're painted blue! I've never seen blue fingernails before. I look down at her feet, and she's wearing the same sneakers as I am, except hers are black and mine are pink.

Class starts, and we don't talk for the rest of the morning. Right before the lunch bell rings, Ms. Moro says, "Sarai, Christina, stop by my desk before you leave." I wonder if she has another letter from Isa. Christina and I walk up to the desk, and Ms. Moro says,

"Sarai, Christina is new here, and I thought it would be great if you could show her around the school today and walk with her over to the cafeteria."

"I'd be happy to," I tell Christina, who nods.

"Let's go." We start walking and Christina still doesn't say anything.

"Where are you from?" I ask her.

"California," she says. "San Diego."

"I've always wanted to go to California!" I say. "Because I love the water. My sister wants to go to Hawaii, but that's even farther away. Did you go to the beach every day in San Diego?"

"No," Christina says.

"Oh," I say. "Well, why did you move to New Jersey? Do you have lots of brothers and sisters? I have two sisters, Lucía and Josie, and I was born here, though my parents weren't." I wait for Christina to say something.

"We moved out here to help take care of my grandma," Christina says. "My mom and I and Wolf."

"Is Wolf your brother?" I ask Christina.

"No," Christina says.

"Is Wolf your . . . sister?" I ask. Christina smiles for the first time.

"She's my dog, Sarai." I really have to listen carefully because her voice is so quiet. "She's awesome. You should meet her sometime."

I'm not sure I want to meet a dog name Wolf, but I don't say that. We walk into the cafeteria, and I need to decide where Christina and I should sit. I start to walk toward my usual table but stop. Christina looks at me. She has reddish-gold eyelashes, and her eyes are blue. I decide to tell her what's going on even though we just met.

"This used to be my favorite table, but there's some not-so-nice girls who sit here now, and they make fun of me," I say, and hesitate. Then Christina says, "Let's find another table, then," and points to a table in the corner.

"Why not?" I say, and we put our backpacks down. "Do you have your cafeteria card?" Christina nods. We walk toward the line, where Lucía is already waiting.

"It's about time!" Lucía says. "I'm starving!"

"Christina," I say, "this is my little sister Lucía. She's in the second grade."

"Hi, Christina!" Lucía says. "Your freckles are so cool! Have you ever counted them? Or named them?"

"No," Christina says, and she smiles for the second time. I smile too.

We eat lunch, and I tell Christina all about my business, Sarai's Sweets, and my dance group, the Playful Primas. I tell her about how I like to sing and dance and perform. She's a good listener. Finally, I ask her, "What do you like to do?"

"Write," she says. She writes for fun? That doesn't sound too exciting to me, but I decide to try and find out more.

"What do you write?" I say, "and where do you write it?" Maybe her old school had a newspaper.

She reaches into her backpack and pulls out a black notebook. In big silver letters, it says:

"That's really cool," I say, and I mean it. We finish our lunch, and I invite her to play on the swings with me. Or maybe join a kickball game.

"No thanks," Christina says. "I need to work on a story." She picks up her notebook and starts writing. I still can't believe Christina would rather sit than play during recess, but I just shrug and say, "Okay," I say. "See you back in class. You know how to get to Ms. Moro's room, right?"

Christina nods without even looking up.

CHAPTER 5

THE BIG ANNOUNCEMENT

When we get back to class, Ms. Moro says, "I have a big announcement to make, students." She stops and smiles, knowing we can't wait to hear what she has to say. "This year, we've decided that MLK Jr. Elementary School will have a talent show!"

"Yeah!" we all cheer. That sounds so fun! As Ms. Moro explains the details, I'm full of ideas that have to do with singing and dancing and acting. I wonder if Lucía and I can do something together.

"We'll have two talent shows, actually, one

for first through third graders, and one for fourth through sixth graders," Ms. Moro explains. I guess I won't be performing with Lucía. Kayla raises her hand.

"Will there be auditions?" Kayla asks. If there are, she doesn't seem too worried about them. I know she dances, like me, but she dances ballet and I dance to modern music. Kayla and I took a ballet class together when we were little, but I didn't like it that much. There were too many rules about where to hold your arms and legs and neck and shoulders and chin. I like to jump around and express myself in my own way, so Mom signed me up for modern and hip-hop dance classes instead. I think Valéria dances ballet at the same studio as Kayla.

"There won't be auditions," Ms. Moro says. "This is a chance for everyone who wants to share their talents. How many of you think you might be interested?" I see Kayla and Valéria raise their hands, and a boy named Auggie, and a few others. I raise my hand too.

"Well," Ms. Moro says, "think about it and let me know by the beginning of next week." The rest of the day goes by fast, and when the bell rings, I'm feeling pretty good. I say goodbye to Christina, and she says goodbye back. As I walk to the bus stop, I think about the day. I didn't get my backpack moved at lunch, and I might have made a new friend. And now I get to plan for the talent show! I spot Lucía at the bus stop, and I'm about to walk toward her when I hear my name called.

"Sarai!" a girl's voice says. I recognize it before I turn around. It's Valéria.

"What?" I ask, and put my hand on my hips. Kayla is standing behind her.

"Are you going to try to perform at the talent show?" they ask.

"I won't be *trying* to perform," I say. "I'll be performing."

"What's your talent?" Kayla asks.

"I'm a dancer and an actress and a singer," I say.

"You dance?" Valéria asks in her snobby way. "You don't LOOK like a dancer."

"What's that supposed to mean?" I say, and I can feel my face getting hot. Just then, Lucía walks up and sort of bumps into Valéria.

"Sorry," Lucía says, but I can tell she's not sorry. "That was an *accident*. Let's go, Sarai."

I turn to walk onto the bus, but then I stop. I turn around to face Valéria and her friends. I use my loudest voice and say, "You know what you need to do to look like a dancer?"

The girls look at me. Valéria is about to say something, but I don't let her. I climb to the top of the bus steps so I'm tallest of all. Then I yell, "Dance!" and snap my fingers at her as the bus doors close.

When Lucía and I get home from school, Tata is waiting as usual, and I ask him if I can write a letter.

"Of course you can, Sarai," he says. "If we walk to the corner store and put it in the mailbox there, it will even go out today!"

"Yay!" says Lucía. She loves walking to Mr. Martinez's store. "Can we get paletas?" she asks. We both love the popsicles Mr. Martínez sells in every yummy flavor—coconut, nuez, mango . . . my favorite is chicle, which is bright blue and bubblegum flavored. There are even little gumballs at the bottom. Lucía likes the nuez flavor because she likes nuts, and Tata chooses a different kind every time we go.

"Thanks, Tata," I say, and go straight into my room and start a letter to Isa because sometimes you just need to talk to your best friend.

Dear Isa,

I'm glad you sent the letter— I was waiting and waiting for you to come back! I still can't believe you had to move. I wish you didn't, but we will definitely be super best pen pals. I hope you like living in Washington, D.C. I'm going to ask if we can drive the rectangle down to visit next summer. I also need to see the monuments and where the president lives because I might run for president some day. You never know.

You asked what's new, and there's not a lot. Valéria and Kayla have been extra mean since you left. I yelled and snapped at them today, and I'm pretty sure my parents wouldn't like that. But sometimes you just have to snap your fingers to prove a point, right?

But here are two good things: 1. There's going to be a talent show at school! And 2. There is a new girl in our class named Christina, and she likes unicorns. She's so quiet I have to bend toward her to hear what she has to say, but so far I like what I hear.

What about you? Have you made any new friends?

Love and awesomeness,
Sarai, your friend forever

I finish the letter and decorate it with stars and unicorns and bring it to my Tata, who has found some stamps. Lucía is dancing in the living room, as usual.

"It's paleta time!" she says.

CHAPTER 6

POPSICLES AND PARTY PLANS

"Hi, Mr. Martínez!" we all say as we walk into his store, Martínez and Sons. I put my letter to Isa in the big blue post office mailbox outside his store. Tata says the last pickup isn't until five o'clock, so the letter will go out today!

"Hola! Hola!" he says with his usual big smile.

"I have an idea," says Lucía. "Let's bring some paletas to the Js' house! I want to see Mama Rosi."

"Me too!" I say. "But we'll have to walk fast so

they don't melt." We buy a rainbow bag of paletas and walk over to the Js' house as fast as we can. Even though Tata has a key, Lucía and I ring the doorbell.

"Surprise!" we say when Mama Rosi opens the door with the twins, Javier and Jade, standing behind her. Lucía and I open up our arms and give Mama Rosi giant abrazos.

"Come in, niñas! I'm so happy to see you," she

says, returning our hugs. Then the twins notice the popsicles and yell.

"Yay!" Javier says. "I want strawberry!"

"I want piña!" Jade says. I hand her the pineapple paleta, and when JuJu comes down the stairs, I give her a high five. Then I hand her a coconut popsicle because I know that's her favorite flavor.

"Thanks!" JuJu says. "Since you guys are here, can we have a Super Awesome Sister-Cousin Fun Club meeting?"

"Why not?" I say.

"But Josie's not here!" says Lucía. Sometimes, Lucía feels sad that Josie misses things because she is in the car so long, but I know Josie and Dad have fun together singing and listening to music on their rides back and forth from school.

"I'll call Dad and tell him we're here, and to come straight over with Josie after school," I say.

"She can make the end of the meeting. I'll save her a paleta too."

"Okay," says Lucía. While I call dad and put a strawberry paleta in the freezer, Mama Rosi shoos the kids into the backyard.

"You are dripping your paletas all over my clean floor!" Mama Rosi says. "Go outside!"

We all go into the backyard and sit at the long red picnic table.

"I call this meeting to order!" I say.

"I do too!" says Lucía. "And if Josie were here she would too!" Josie, Lucía, and I are co-presidents of the club. It was the only way they would agree to join because according to them, I act like the boss too much.

"I have an order of business," says JuJu. "It's about the weekend. It's supposed to be really sunny."

"I like the sun," says Jade.

"Me too," says, Javier, licking his paleta. The twins are so cute. They're six years old and full of energy. I doubt they'll make it through the whole meeting.

"So I thought maybe we could have a picnic at the park after church," JuJu says. "And then plan something fun."

"Like kickball?" Lucía asks. "Or tag?"

"Even more fun than that . . ." says JuJu.

"Nothing's more fun than tag," Lucía says. "I like to catch people." And does she ever. Playing tag with Lucía gets interesting because she seems to think that tagging someone means knocking them down. Mom and Dad say she doesn't know her own strength, but I'm not so sure about that.

"How about creative ideas?" JuJu says.

"Like art?" Jade says, and like a lightning bolt, a thought hits me.

"I know!" I say, raising my finger and pointing to the sky. "Let's play rainbow . . . art . . . paint . . . tag!" Everyone looks at me. "We'll get white T-shirts and set up bowls of tempera paint in every color of the rainbow. There can be taggers and runners. The first person to get paint of every color on their shirt wins!"

"Yes!" says Lucía.

"I like that idea," says Javier.

"So when you get tagged you are out?" asks

Jade. "That won't be very fun for the first person who gets tagged."

"Maybe not," says JuJu. "Maybe when you are tagged you have to do something, and then you get to run again."

"Like jumping jacks?" says Javier.

"That's perfect!" I say. "If you get tagged, you have to do five jumping jacks before you can run again."

We talk more about the rules and how we'll use some of the money from our chicha morada stand to buy white T-shirts and pretty soon we've got a plan for the best game ever.

"I'm the co-president, and I say it's time for a vote!" Lucía says. "All in favor?"

We all raise our hands.

"It's a plan!" I say. "This Sunday afternoon will be the first annual Rainbow Art Paint Tag Event!"

CHAPTER 7

RAINBOW TAG

The next day, Christina and I sit together at lunch again, and I learn a little more about her. I ask her lots of questions, and her answers get a little longer. I think she's just quiet, not shy. I find out Christina's favorite colors are black and green, and tell her that mine are hot pink and lavender. She doesn't just love unicorns, she loves dragons too.

"Are there dragons in your book?" I ask.

"Not in this book, but definitely in my next one," she says.

"Do you really think unicorns are real?" I ask her. "I mean, I know they're real in your stories."

"Well, there have been unicorns in art for hundreds of years. Not always like horses, but sometimes looking like goats or antelopes," Christina says. "I've done research at the library."

"The library!" I say. "That reminds me. You haven't met Ms. Milligan, the most awesome librarian ever! You'll meet her Friday, but instead of going outside, why don't we go and say hi before the bell?"

"Sure," Christina says, and off we go.

"Ms. Milligan!" I say, walking into the library. There aren't any classes in the library during lunch, so I figure I can be as loud as I want.

"Hi, Sarai," Ms. Milligan says, from behind her desk. I see she's eating lunch. "What kind of sandwich are you having?"

"Peanut butter and banana," Ms. Milligan says.

"I didn't know you like peanut butter and banana sandwiches, Ms. Milligan," I say. "I thought teachers only ate boring stuff."

"Never!" she says, pointing to her mug. "I'm having cinnamon hot chocolate too. My own special recipe."

"Yum! I like sweets things too. We have a lot in common," I tell Ms. Milligan.

"Why don't you introduce me to your new

friend?" Ms. Milligan says. Whoops. Christina is so quiet I almost forgot about her.

"This is Christina! She's new and she's from San Diego and she likes unicorns and dragons," I say.

"Hi, Christina." Ms. Milligan smiles. "Welcome to Martin Luther King, Jr. Elementary! I'll see you on Friday, and we can find some books you'll enjoy. We have lots of fantasy novels." Christina nods and looks around at the big library. We walk around, and I show her the bean bags. Then the bell rings, and we head to class.

I sit with Christina at lunch on Thursday and Friday. Every day I like her a little more. She's a good listener. I tell her about my talent show dilemma. "I don't know whether to sing or dance or try something new like acting. And if I act, what will I act out?"

Christina surprises me by saying, "If you want to act, I can help you write something."

"Really?" I say. "Like a play? Will you be in it?"

"No, but I could write a story or poem just for you," Christina says, "and you could act out all the parts."

"That would be super awesome! But the show is in two weeks. When will we work on it?"

"We can work on it during lunch," she says, "and recess." I like to run around during recess, but it sounds like so much fun to work with someone on a project that I say, "Okay!" and then I add, "My family is playing rainbow art paint tag at Roberto Clemente Park this Sunday afternoon. Do you want to come? We could talk about the story after we play tag."

"Tag?" Christina says, frowning. "I don't really like tag."

"Oh," I say, a little disappointed. "But the park is really cool. It has awesome play sets and lots of grass. It's named after the famous Puerto Rican baseball player." Christina doesn't look very impressed. "Don't you like running around or playing sports?" I ask her.

"Not really," Christina says.

"How about dancing?" I ask.

"Definitely not," Christina says.

"Then how do you exercise?" I ask.

"I walk my dog every morning and afternoon," Christina says.

"Oh," I say. "Some people bring their dogs to the park." I don't say anything more. I've never

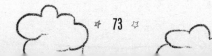

met anyone who writes during recess or who doesn't like to go the park. I think of Isa and how we liked all the same things, and all of a sudden I really miss her.

On Sunday, Josie, Lucía, and I are super wiggly at church. We are so excited about paint tag. JuJu picked up the shirts and paint at Jack's Art Shack, and I have a bunch of plastic bowls and Frisbees in the back of the rectangle—our minivan. Mom and Dad packed a picnic lunch, and we drive to Roberto Clemente Park as soon as services are over. When we arrive, the Js are already there, along with Tío Miguel, Tía Sofía, and my grandparents Tata and Mama Rosi. It looks like Javier's friend Calvin is there too. JuJu runs right up to me.

"Everything is ready!" she says. "We just need to figure out what the safe bases are."

"I thought we could use Frisbees as safe bases," I say. Together we put them around the field. JuJu and the twins have set up five "paint" areas spread far apart.

"We don't have music, Josie, because Tata hasn't fixed the boom box yet," Jade says.

"That's okay," Josie signs and says.

"Okay, everyone," I say, "it's time to start. Put on your T-shirts." Most of the T-shirts reach down to our knees—below the knees on Lucía and the twins.

"The big sizes were on sale," JuJu explains.

"Good!" Tía Sofía says, laughing. "Then you'll get less paint on your clothes."

"You look like little ghosts!" Tata says.

"Not for long," I say. "And don't worry, Tía Sofía, I know from experience that tempera washes off."

Dad offers to be the tagger.

"I'm ready to start chasing ghosts!" Dad says. "I'm the fastest thing on two legs!"

"No, you aren't!" says Lucía. "I am!" We all walk out into the center of the field.

"Okay, Josie, you do the honors," I say.

"Ready, set, go!" she signs and says. And we are off. Dad chases, and we run and get tagged and do jumping jacks and run again and dip our fingers and hands in paint and pretty soon we are all rainbow-colored messes. We end up forgetting all the rules, and pretty soon everyone is running everywhere and trying to paint and tag each other. That includes Dad, and he doesn't even have on a special shirt! Everybody laughs, nobody wins, and our shirts look awesome! We run around until we can't anymore and then Mom comes over to take a picture.

"Okay, everyone, get in a group," she says. And we decide that a pyramid will look cool, and we try to make one with me, JuJu, Josie, and Calvin on the bottom, then the twins, then Lucía. It sort of works, and Mom gets the picture before we all come tumbling down.

We're eating lunch, when I see two people walking toward us. It's Christina! And the redheaded lady must be her mom. And they have a dog. It's little and black and looks like a stuffed animal. I run up to Christina.

"This is Wolf?" I ask, laughing and bending to pet him.

"Yup," Christina says, smiling. "And this is my mom."

"Hi, Ms. McKay," I say, "nice to meet you."

"Call me Kathy," she says, and smiles. I notice that she has just as many freckles as Christina. "Christina told me all about you, and we thought we'd stop by and say hi."

"Come meet my family," I say. My mom and dad start talking to Ms. McKay, and my sisters and cousins are excited about Wolf. I introduce Christina to the group.

"These are my cousins, JuJu, Javier, Jade, and

Jade's friend Calvin, and my sisters, Lucía, who you've met, and Josie, who you haven't. That's my Tío Miguel, my Tía Sofía, my Tata, and my Mama. Rosi." I take a big breath. "Everyone! This is my new friend Christina from San Diego. She's awesome," I say, and I mean it.

CHAPTER 8

THE BIG SHOW

Christina and I work on the talent show script together every day at lunch, and she even comes over the next weekend. I spend some time inside Christina's world of unicorns and dragons, and I like it there. We don't tell anybody but our teacher, Ms. Moro, what we are going to do for the talent show.

Finally, the big day arrives, and it feels like my stomach is doing jumping jacks. The talent show is first thing in the morning!

"Good luck, darling, you'll do great," Mom says before she leaves for work.

"It will be awesome!" Dad agrees. "I only wish I could be there." Mom and Dad give me extra-long hugs and then Lucía and I are off to the bus stop.

I peek out at the audience from behind the stage.

"Get back," I hear Valéria hiss. "It's not your turn!"

"Well, it's not yours *either*," I say. "I just wanted to see how many kids are out there." All the performers are waiting backstage, and Auggie has just finished performing. The audience is clapping super loud, and I know why. He's great. I've gone to school with him for years, and I had no idea he could play the drums like that! He takes a bow and walks backstage, right by Valéria, Kayla, and me. We are the last two acts.

"Great job!" I tell Auggie.

"Thanks," he says, smiling.

"We're next," Valéria tells me. "So watch and learn." Kayla laughs, as usual, but I notice she looks a little scared. I can relate. Where's Christina anyways? She's supposed to be backstage to help me get ready to perform her poem. I search for her, and sure enough, she's sitting in a corner . . . *writing*.

"Christina! How can you write at a time like this?" I say. "I'm nervous." Christina closes her journal, looks up, and smiles.

"Why?" she asks. "You'll do great."

"Quick! Give me the lines to read again. What if I forget one?"

"You don't need to go over the lines again," Christina says. "We practiced and practiced. You know them perfectly."

"Okay," I say, and I hear Ms. Moro say,

"Our next act is titled 'Butterfly Ballet,' to be danced by Valéria Ruiz and Kayla Green."

I look to the stage. Even I have to admit that Kayla and Valéria look cool. They have on sparkly wings and matching leotards. They start to dance, and it's really neat. I see Kayla forget a few steps, and I actually wince. Valéria won't like that at all. Still, they do a really good job, and when they finish, there's loud applause. They walk offstage toward me. Kayla looks relieved, but Valéria looks mad. I don't have time to think about it, though, because it's time! I watch Ms. Moro walk up to the microphone. I see my sister Lucía in the audience. Dad lent her his phone, and she's ready to start recording my performance.

"Our next act," Ms. Moro says, "is titled 'Septima the Unicorn and Diego Dragón,' written by Christina McKay and performed by Sarai Gonzalez."

That's my cue. I walk out to the center of the stage and take a deep breath. I've practiced my voices, and it's time to bring Christina's words to life.

Once upon a time, in a cave on a hill,
There lived a magic unicorn named Septima Seville.
Septima galloped and played on the mountainside,
Offering children and parents unicorn rides.
The people of the village loved the unicorn,
With her beautiful tail and enchanted horn.
But all was not well in the village fair,
And Septima smelled the fear and worry in the air.
The children were afraid of Diego Dragón,
With his breath of fire and his burning tongue.
Diego Dragón would bare his teeth, screech, and yell
Until, to their knees, the frightened children fell.
One day, Septima followed Diego's flight
And saw the tears falling from his eyes at night.
"You may be a dragon," she said. "You're fierce and strong,
But you need a friend, I can't be wrong."
"Talk," Septima advised, "don't screech and shout.
Share your pain, instead of striking out."
"It's my throat, it burns," Diego finally said.
"The fire just won't stop inside my head."
"Let me help and ask the sky to ease your pain,"
Septima said, and used her magic to make it rain.
The healing water fell and put Diego's fire out,
And Septima and Diego danced and pranced about.
They romped joyfully in Dandelion Park,
Laughing and talking until it was nearly dark.
Diego Dragón learned to play and be kind
From a unicorn with a magical mind.
And, of course, the place this enchanted story ends
Is with Septima and Diego Dragón becoming best of friends!

I end the performance with a whirl and a swirl and a deep bow. For a second, it's silent, and then it sounds like EVERYONE claps. Loudly. I hear Lucía cheer, but she's not the only one. I look to the side of the stage, and Christina is smiling and giving me a thumbs-up. I wave at her and tell her to come out. She shakes her head. I walk over to her and take her hand, and finally she comes out from behind the curtains for a quick bow. We go back to our seats to watch the rest of the show.

Finally, at the end of the show, Ms. Moro walks up onstage to announce the winners. I grip Christina's hand.

She leans into the microphone and says,

"Our third-place winners today are . . . Valéria Ruiz and Kayla Green!" I let out a breath. I watch Valéria and Kayla march up onstage to get their certificate. Valéria doesn't even smile, though Kayla does and thanks Ms. Moro.

"Next," Ms. Moro continues, "I am very happy to announce our second-place winners . . . Sarai Gonzalez and Christina McKay!"

"Yay!" I say, and I grab Christina's hand and we go up onstage. I can hear Lucía shouting and people clapping, and I feel like I'm floating on a cloud. The next thing I know, I'm hearing Ms. Moro announce Auggie Chavez as the winner and more cheering and more high fives. I am happy Christina and I got second, and I feel proud. I barely notice Valéria and Kayla, who seem annoyed.

Later that day, in the cafeteria at lunch, Christina and I leave our backpacks at our new table in the corner. When we get back, my backpack is gone, and Valéria, Kayla, and the rest of their friends are sitting there.

"Where's my backpack?" I ask Valéria.

"Wouldn't you like to know?" she replies, and

then turns to Christina. "Christina, we saved you a seat. You should join us."

"We loved your poem," Kayla says. "It was amazing."

"It was awesome," Valéria says, "but we still should have won the talent show. In any case, come hang out with us." I look at Christina, and she's not saying anything and just when I think she's going to sit down at the table with them, she shakes her head.

"No, thanks," she says. "Now tell us where Sarai's backpack is and move. This is *our* table."

"You wish," says Valéria, and turns back to her friends.

Christina grabs my hand and pulls me away from the table. She looks at me and says, "We need to tell the teacher."

"You realize they will call us tattletales, right?" I say.

"We aren't tattletales—we are whistle-blowers!" Christina says.

"You mean, like a referee blowing a whistle when someone fouls?"

"That's right," Christina agrees.

"We aren't tattling—we are whistling!" I say, and together we go to find Ms. Moro. She comes and talks to Valéria and her friends, and they tell us where my backpack is. I tell her about all the other times it's happened, and Valéria and Kayla are benched for recess and warned that they can't move other people's things without their permission. There will be no more moving of backpacks. Before Christina and I leave for recess, Kayla stops me.

"Sarai," she says. "I'm sorry about your backpack. And you're performance was awesome."

"Thanks," I say. "So was yours." Christina and I go out to the playground. She sits on a bench and opens her notebook, and I run off to play on the monkey bars but not before we give each other a big hug. Today is a good day.

CHAPTER 9

OLD FRIENDS

The mail comes on Saturday morning, and it turns out I have a letter from Isa. I am so excited to open it.

Dear Sarai,

I was so happy to get your letter! I miss you so much. I'm sorry that Valéria and her friends are being mean. They are just jealous because you're Sarai, you're awesome, and you aren't afraid of anything!

How did the talent show go? Did you sing or dance? How's Ms. Moro? I miss her, though my new teacher, Ms. Smith, is funny and nice.

I'm glad the new girl is cool. Unicorns are pretty. I've made a couple new friends at school, and it's cool because the family next door to us has lots of kids to play with. One of the kids is in my class at school, and he's really fun. He likes soccer a lot, so I've been playing lots of soccer at recess. Most of my friends here are boys, but so what?

Even if you can't come to D.C., I will still see you because Mom and Dad say we will be back soon to visit.

Love from your super best pen pal,

Isa Lopez, future soccer star!

P.S. Write back soon!

Dear Isa:

Wow, Isa Lopez, soccer star! It's fun to try new things, isn't it? For the talent show, I didn't sing or dance. I acted. It was super awesome, and my new friend, Christina, and I came in second place. She wrote a story about a unicorn and a dragon, and I performed it.

When you come visit, I want you to meet Christina. She doesn't like to run around or dance or sing, but she likes other cool things and I've figured out that friends can be different from each other. I think you'll like Christina too. It's awesome that you have friends that are boys. The important thing is having friends.

It's funny that you said I'm not afraid of anything. The truth is, I am. I'm afraid of spiders and not being able to be myself, and when you left, I was afraid I wouldn't make new friends. But guess what? I've decided that making new friends is NOT something to be afraid of. Not now. Not ever. And keeping old friends too is pretty awesome too.

Love from your super best pen pal,
Sarai Gonzalez,
actress, singer, dancer, baker, and cupcake maker
P.S. Write back SOON!

BFFs

SARAI GONZALEZ
AND MONICA BROWN

SCHOLASTIC